A Beginning-to-Read Book

I Love You, Dear Dragon

by Margaret Hillert

Illustrated by Carl Kock

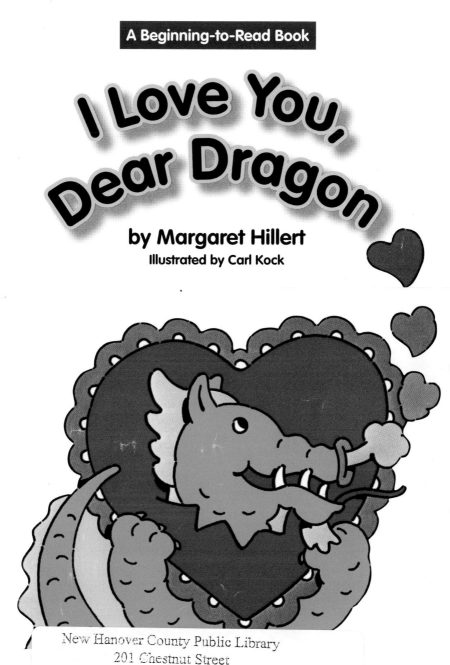

DEAR CAREGIVER,

The *Beginning-to-Read* series is a carefully written collection of classic readers you may remember from your own childhood. Each book features text comprised of common sight words to provide your child ample practice reading the words that appear most frequently in written text. The many additional details in the pictures enhance the story and offer the opportunity for you to help your child expand oral language and develop comprehension.

Begin by reading the story to your child, followed by letting him or her read familiar words and soon your child will be able to read the story independently. At each step of the way, be sure to praise your reader's efforts to build his or her confidence as an independent reader. Discuss the pictures and encourage your child to make connections between the story and his or her own life. At the end of the story, you will find reading activities and a word list that will help your child practice and strengthen beginning reading skills.

Above all, the most important part of the reading experience is to have fun and enjoy it!

Shannon Cannon

Shannon Cannon,
Literacy Consultant

Norwood House Press • P.O. Box 316598 • Chicago, Illinois 60631
For more information about Norwood House Press please visit our website at
www.norwoodhousepress.com or call 866-565-2900.

LIBRARY OF CONGRESS CATALOGING-IN-PUBLICATION DATA

Hillert, Margaret.
 I love you, dear dragon / by Margaret Hillert ; illustrated by Carl Kock.—
Rev. and expanded library ed.
  p. cm.
 Summary: A boy and his pet dragon celebrate Valentine's Day by noticing all the red things they see, making Valentines, and eating a Valentine cake. Includes reading activities.
 ISBN-13: 978-1-59953-020-8 (library edition : alk. paper)
 ISBN-10: 1-59953-020-1 (library edition : alk. paper)
 1. Readers (Primary) [1. Readers.] I. Kock, Carl, ill. II. Title.
PE1119.H57875 2006
428.6—dc22   2005033944

Red, red, red.
I like red.
Red is pretty.

3

Look up here.
Here is something red.
Little and red.

It is pretty.
It wants something to eat.
We can help it.

Oh, oh, oh.
Here is something red.
Something big, big and red.

Look at it go.
It can help.
It can do good work.

And look up here.
Look up, up, up.
This is red, too.

It can help us.
Do not go.
Look and look.

Now we can go.
Run, run, run.
But look out, too.

Here is something big and red.
I work in here.
I play here, too.

Here we are.
Mother wants something in here.
Something red.
We will look for it.

Can we find it?
Yes, yes.
This is it.
This is what we want.

Mother, Mother.
Here we are.
Here is what you want.

Here is one for you to eat.
And here is one for you.
It is good for you and pretty, too.

Look who is here
with something for us.
What is it?
Guess what it is.

Oh, look at it.
It is pretty.
It is red.
"I love you" is on it.

We can make something
like this.
Do it like this.
Work, work, work.

See here, Mother.
See what we can make.
Do you like it?

I do. I do.
But see what I can make for you.
Something to eat.

Oh, my.
This is good.
Good, good, good!
We like it.

And we like what Father can do.
This is fun.
Good fun for us.

Here you are with me.
And here I am with you.
I love you.
I love you, dear dragon.

The following activities support the findings of the National Reading Panel that determined the most effective components for reading instruction are: Phonemic Awareness, Phonics, Vocabulary, Fluency, and Text Comprehension.

Phonemic Awareness: The /r/ sound

Sound Substitution: Say the words on the left to your child. Ask your child to repeat the word, changing the first sound to /**r**/:

pat = rat	cut = rut	sip = rip
man = ran	cap = rap	lake = rake
fun = run	night = right	

Phonics: The letter Rr

1. Demonstrate how to form the letters **R** and **r** for your child.

2. Have your child practice writing **R** and **r** at least three times each.

3. Ask your child to point to the words in the book that start with the letter **r**.

4. Write down the following words and ask your child to circle the letter **r** in each word:

rat	car	ran	rug	bar	dragon	red
run	start	rice	jar	race	cart	bread

Vocabulary: Naming Objects

1. Ask your child to name the red objects in the story.

2. Write the words on sticky notes and have the child place them next to the objects on the correct pages.

3. Add the sentence starter "It is a..." in front of the words on the sticky notes.

4. Reread the story with your child and insert the new sentences. For example, page 4 might now read,

> Look up here.
> Here is something red.
> Little and red.
> *It is a bird.*

Fluency: Echo Reading

1. Reread the story to your child at least two more times while your child tracks the print by running a finger under the words as they are read. Ask your child to read the words he or she knows with you.

2. Reread the story, stopping after each sentence or page to allow your child to read (echo) what you have read. Repeat echo reading and let your child take the lead.

Text Comprehension: Discussion Time

1. Ask your child to retell the sequence of events in the story.

2. To check comprehension, ask your child the following questions:

   • What red object did the postal worker deliver?

   • What are boy and his father doing on pages 26-27? How do you think they are feeling? Why?

   • What is your favorite color and what are some things that are your favorite color?

WORD LIST

***I Love You, Dear Dragon* uses the 60 words listed below.**
This list can be used to practice reading the words that appear in the text.
You may wish to write the words on index cards and use them to help your
child build automatic word recognition. Regular practice with these words
will enhance your child's fluency in reading connected text.

am	go	not	up
and	good	now	us
are	guess		
at		oh	want(s)
	help	on	we
big	here	one	what
but		out	who
	I		will
can	in	play	with
come(s)	is	pretty	work
	it		
dear		red	yes
do	like	run	you
dragon	little		
	look	see	
eat	love	something	
father		this	
find	make	to	
for	man	too	
fun	me		
	mother		
	my		

ABOUT THE AUTHOR Margaret Hillert has written over 80 books for
children who are just learning to read. Her books
have been translated into many different languages and over a million children
throughout the world have read her books. She first started writing poetry as
a child and has continued to write for children and adults throughout her life. A
first grade teacher for 34 years, Margaret is now retired from teaching and lives in
Michigan where she likes to write, take walks in the morning, and care for her three cats.

Photograph by Glenna Washburn

ABOUT THE ADVISER Shannon Cannon contributed the activities pages that appear in
this book. Shannon serves as a literacy consultant and provides
staff development to help improve reading instruction. She is a frequent presenter at educational
conferences and workshops. Prior to this she worked as an elementary school teacher and as
president of a curriculum publishing company.

MG   11/06